HOOSIER CADDIE

A Novel Tale by

Rick King

Published by: USA Publishing Hub

www.USApublishinghub.com

To the clubhouse workers of Foster Park Golf Course—Dick Melton, Donny Schnagle, and the many others who have walked its halls, worked its counters, and shared its stories.

Your camaraderie, humor, and passion for the game inspired this story, and I hope it honors the spirit of those who make the course more than just a place to play.

And to my beautiful wife, Cindy—thank you for believing in me, encouraging me, and putting up with my frustrations along the way. This wouldn't have been possible without you.

A TOAST

To Those Who Walk the Fairways
With steady hands and knowing eyes,
Through morning mists and sunlit skies,
The caddie walks, a guiding light,
A silent partner in the fight.
The golfer dreams, the shot takes flight,
A game of patience earned by might.
Through wind and rain, through loss and gain,
They chase the course; they bear the strain.
So, here's to those who love the game,
Who seek the flag, who call its name.
With heart and grit, they stand with pride,
Through every swing—side by side.

INTRODUCTION

"Let me tell ye a tale about the wild world of caddying in the heart of the Hoosier State. Many a golfer has braved the lush greens and rolling fairways of Fort Wayne's beautiful courses, but few have truly mastered the art of the game. That's where I come in—an old Scotsman with a keen eye for the ball and an even keener wit.

Caddying, ye see, is no job for the faint-hearted. On the course, yer not just carryin' clubs; yer carryin' dreams, tempers, and sometimes heartbreak. Me? I learned the ropes the hard way, stumbling through mistakes and triumphs alike, but every step was worth it. I've seen it all, from novice hackers to seasoned pros, and I've got a story or two to share. So, grab your clubs and your sense of humor, and let's tee off on this grand adventure together!

Now, ya might be askin' yerselves, 'Why do I need a sense of humor?' Ha! Without it, you're bound to hate yer game. Golf is a fickle mistress. She'll seduce ye with her beauty, pull ye in with promises of glory, then cut ye down to size the moment ye think yer in control. Trust me, if ye don't learn to laugh at yerself, ye might as well take up bowling.

I'm Gavin McTavish, born in North Berwick, Scotland, way back in the 1940s. It's a seaside town in East Lothian, about 45 minutes east of Edinburgh. North Berwick has postcard beauty, with its harbor dotted with boats, stunning Victorian villas, and fish-and-chip shops wafting their salty aroma through the air. It's a wee bit reminiscent of St. Andrews—a true gem of a place steeped in golf history. They've been teeing it up at the North Berwick Golf Club since the 17th century, and my father was a greenskeeper before the war started. I spent more time on the course than anywhere else, toddling about before I was two.

We left Scotland after the war—World War II—and made our way to the United States, to a little place called Fort Wayne, Indiana. It wasn't an easy move, mind ye. Imagine trading the rugged cliffs and salty air of Scotland for the flat plains of the Midwest. But Mum, a surgical nurse, found work at the local hospital, and Dad got a job at the Foster Park Golf Course as part of the grounds crew.

Foster Park was where I swung my first club, and it became my escape, my teacher, and my playground. By the time I was 15, I knew every inch of that course like the back of my hand. Golf was in my blood, and Foster Park was where my love for the game truly took root. It's where I learned the art of caddying, where I carried not just clubs but the weight of dreams—mine and others'.

This is my story, and it's not just about golf. It's about life, hard work, laughter, and the lessons learned on the fairways and greens of Indiana. So, let's set off together on this journey. Just remember to keep yer grip strong, yer head down, and yer sense of humor sharp."

Table of Contents

CHAPTER 1

The Beginning

When I was just a wee lad in Scotland, the world was at war. WWII was raging, and every man between the ages of 18 and 51 was called to serve. My dad was no exception. He was drafted into the Royal Scotts Regiment, leaving behind my mother and I…I was too young to understand what was happening, but I knew enough to realize that my world had suddenly changed.

Scotland played a significant role in the war—a hub of industry, intelligence, and manufacturing that made us both valuable and vulnerable. The Germans knew this, and their air raids often targeted Scottish cities and shipyards. The sound of sirens wailing in the dead of the night became a part of life. Even as a child, I understood the fear that gripped our town when the skies darkened with enemy aircraft.

My mother, a surgical nurse, was one of the strongest women I ever knew. Our days started before the sun even had a chance to rise. She had to be at the hospital by six in the morning, which meant an early start for the both of us. She'd wake me, feed me, dress me, and walk me to my grandmother's house before making the mile-long trek to work, regardless of the weather. After a long shift at the hospital, she'd return to my grandmother's, eat supper with me, then take me home, give me a bath, and tell me a bedtime story before collapsing into bed—only to do it all over again the next day.

She never complained, never faltered.

As I grew, she taught me how to be independent. By the time I was in school, I knew how to cook simple meals, clean up after myself, sew on a button, and do a hundred other things most boys my age hadn't even thought about. Mom was my rock, my protector, my entire world.

Then, one day in the middle of my second-grade year, the war ended.

Our town of North Berwick erupted in celebration. People flooded the streets, cheering, hugging, crying tears of joy and relief. I didn't fully understand the weight of the moment—I just knew that everyone around me was happy. When I arrived home, I saw a man in uniform sitting on our porch. His hat was pulled low over his eyes, but when he lifted his head, I recognized him instantly.

It was my dad.

Tears welled up in my eyes, and I ran to him as fast as my little legs would carry me. He caught me in a hug so tight I thought I was going to burst.

"Aye, tha's my boy!" he said, his voice thick with emotion. "My, how you've grown!"

That night, sitting at the dinner table with both my parents for the first time in years, I felt whole again. We laughed, we talked, we celebrated. But there was something different about Dad. His laughter didn't come as easily as it once had, and sometimes I'd catch him staring off into the distance, lost in thought. I'd ask him about the war, but he always shook his head and said, "I'll tell ya when you're older."

Life slowly returned to normal—at least, as normal as it could be. Dad took a job as a greenskeeper at the local golf course, and every day after school, I'd go there to be near him. I'd sit under a big oak tree, doing my homework while he worked on the course. When school was out for the summer, I'd spend every waking hour there, running across the fairways, watching the golfers, fascinated by the game.

But times were still tough. Scotland's economy struggled in the years after the war. Industries like coal mining and shipbuilding, once the backbone of our economy, were declining, leaving thousands unemployed. One night, my parents sat me down at the dinner table for a serious conversation.

"We're going on an adventure," Mom said with a smile.

Two weeks later, we were standing on the docks, saying good-bye to my grandmother, boarding a massive ship bound for the United States of America.

I was too young to understand the gravity of what was happening. To me, it really did feel like an adventure. I didn't grasp that we were leaving behind everything we had ever known. I didn't know then that we would never return.

A New Life in America

When we arrived in the States, Mom had already secured a job at St. Joseph Hospital as a nurse, and Dad eventually found work with the city's Parks & Recreation Department. He was assigned as a greenskeeper at the Foster Park Golf Course—the oldest public course in the city.

I'll never forget the first time I saw it.

Foster Park was breathtaking. The park spanned 276 acres, with lush gardens, a playground, and a river walk that wound its way around the fairways. The golf course itself was stunning, with rolling greens, towering trees, and a timeless beauty that seemed almost magical.

We lived nearby, which meant I could walk to both school and the golf course. It didn't take long before I was spending nearly all my free time at the course, watching Dad work, soaking in the sights and sounds of the game. I was still too little to play, but I was mesmerized by the golfers—the way they carried themselves, the way they studied their shots, the way the ball soared through the air like a bird in flight.

That's when I first noticed the loopers.

The caddies.

They were older boys, carrying the heavy bags of the golfers, reading greens, offering advice, and getting paid for it. They walked the course as if they belonged there, and in a way, they did. They weren't just carrying clubs; they were part of the game itself.

I wanted to be one of them.

I had no idea then that caddying would change my life forever.

Chapter 2

The Looper

It was 1957 when I first started to caddie. I was 12 years old. Back then, they called us "loopers." We'd gather at the course, sit on the wooden bench, and wait for a golfer to hire us. For a dollar, we'd carry their clubs for 18 holes, often making three or four loops in a day.

I met all the regulars and caddied for most at one time or another. My favorite was a guy named Fredrick. He always paid me with four quarters and bought me a Coke after the round. One day, he said, "I've got a gift for you." He handed me six golf clubs. "These were mine when I was about your age," he said. "It's not a whole set, and they've got some age on 'em, but it'll help you learn the game." I thanked him happily. It was like being given a treasure. I practiced every day and caddied as much as I could.

John Sonnerburg was the pro at Foster Park Golf Course then. He was always kind to me, helping improve my golf game and sharing tips to be a better caddie. He was happy to see me have some clubs and even gave me a golf bag to carry them in.

One day, he asked me to loop for him during the upcoming Fort Wayne City Championship.

"Sure!" I said immediately, though I didn't know much about caddying for tournaments. But I loved the game and knew the course like the back of my hand.

The tournament was six weeks away. After school, I'd meet John to watch him practice. My job was to record every shot he made, catalog the distances of his clubs, and memorize the breaks and slopes of every green. John was meticulous, and I followed his lead, eager to learn.

My dad got wind of my plan and asked me, "So, how much is he payin' ya?"

I hesitated. "I dunno."

With a sharp swat from a rolled-up newspaper, he shouted, "I dinna raise ya to work for free! If you're gonna work, you deserve to get paid!"

The next day, I approached John before practice. "Me dad asked what you're paying me for the tournament," I said nervously.

Dad's words echoed in my head: *If you're gonna work, you deserve to get paid!* But this wasn't just about money. This was about showing John—and myself—that I wasn't just some kid tagging along for fun. I wanted him to see me as someone who could handle the pressure, someone who belonged on this course.

I didn't just want the money. I *needed* it. Dad had been talking about getting me a set of clubs for my birthday, but I knew we couldn't afford it. If I could put something toward it, maybe I'd show him I wasn't just a kid waiting for handouts.

I swallowed hard, my palms sweaty. It wasn't the money I cared about—not really. What I wanted was for John to see me as more than a kid with a thick accent and a head full of dreams. If I could stand my ground here, maybe he'd see I was someone worth betting on.

John chuckled, leaning on the counter. "What's this, Mac? You planning to buy a car with your tournament earnings?"

I flushed but didn't back down. "No, sir. I just think if I'm gonna do the job right, I should be paid fair for it."

His grin faded, and for the first time, I saw him looking at me like an equal. "Fair enough, Mac. Let's talk terms."

This wasn't just about one tournament. If I could do this—really prove myself—who's to say what else I could do? Maybe one day, I'd get to play in tournaments, not just carry the bag. But first, I had to show John I could handle this.

Seeing me lost in thought, John chuckled. "I'll pay you five bucks guaranteed, or you can take ten percent of my bet winnings."

"How much is that?" I asked.

"Well," he said with a grin, "I've got two hundred bucks in bets. If I win, you'd make twenty. If I lose, you'd get nothing—same as me."

I thought it over. "I'll take the five bucks guaranteed."

"Smart choice," he said, shaking my hand.

For the next five weeks, we worked harder than ever. I memorized his distances, calculated wind directions, and walked every green to study the breaks.

Two days before the tournament, John surprised me and said we'd be playing a full practice round—all 18 holes. "You know what to do, and this will make it more real."

"Mac," he said, "I don't want you to be nervous. Hand me the clubs, call the wind, and tell me where to aim. Got it?"

"Got it, boss."

"Don't call me boss," he snapped. "You're my caddie, not my servant. Call me John."

The first hole was a long par 4 with trees on the right and thick rough on the left. I handed him his 3-wood.

"Wind's at your back, eight miles an hour. You'll hit it 250, leaving 175 to the pin—a perfect 6-iron approach," I said.

He chuckled and nailed the shot, dead center at 250 yards.

By the 9th hole, he was four under par, and I was struggling to keep up. Carrying a heavy pro bag and clubs wasn't easy for a kid my size.

"Are you ready to call it quits?" John asked, seeing me struggle.

"Nah, I'll be fine," I said, though I wasn't so sure.

At the turn, John bought me a hot dog and a Coke. It was the best meal I'd ever had. As we ate, I asked John how I was doing.

He grinned and said, "Well, you know the course, you're a natural at reading the greens, and you sure know my club distances, but I think my bag is too heavy."

"I'll be fine," I said.

We finished the back nine, but it was tough. John hit two bad shots and missed a putt, getting a triple bogey on 10, then proceeded to get three more bogeys. That's where I learned you can't let one bad shot turn into eight bad shots. "Keep your head in the game and focus on your strengths."

As we were leaving, John said, "Let's take tomorrow off, and I'll see you Thursday. Don't be late—I'm counting on you!"

The next day, I left early and headed to the course. My dad and the rest of the grounds crew were preparing the course for the tournament—changing the tee boxes, defining the fairways, rolling the greens, and changing the hole placements. I took my time and walked each hole, marking in my caddie book each distance and where the hazards would be. By the time I finished, I knew I could handle it.

The Tournament Day 1 – A Strong Start

The first day of the Fort Wayne City Championship dawned perfect—blue skies, a slight breeze, and the kind of crisp morning air that made you believe anything was possible. Foster Park was alive with energy as golfers checked in, exchanged handshakes, and eyed the competition. The smell of fresh-cut grass mixed with the aroma of coffee and cigars as the gallery gathered near the first tee.

John was ready. Focused. He had been playing some of the best golf of his life, and I was determined to do my part. As his caddie, I knew my job wasn't just to carry his bag—it was to keep him steady, to make sure he stayed locked in from the first tee shot to the final putt.

John started strong, firing a three-under 67. By the end of the day, he was tied for the lead with Ken Rodewald and Tom Kelly, two of the best golfers in town. As we walked off the 18th green, he gave me a wink.

"Mac, you did great today," he said, slapping me on the back. "You've got a real knack for this. I'm glad I've got you on my bag."

I grinned, shaking his hand. "Thanks! I think we've got what it takes to win this."

John nodded. "We'll do our best."

I believed him.

Day 2 – The Elements Strike Back

The weather turned overnight. The morning sky was gray, thick with clouds, and by the time we teed off, the rain had started—a steady drizzle that soaked the fairways and made every step heavier. The wind picked up, swirling unpredictably, turning what had been a golfer's paradise into a battlefield.

But John didn't flinch. If anything, he thrived in the adversity.

He moved through the course with laser focus, his eyes scanning every shot like a hawk searching for prey. While others struggled, John adapted. He carved low shots through the wind, played safe when needed, and attacked when the opportunity was right. When he drained a 20-foot birdie putt on 18, he clenched his fist in quiet triumph.

A four-under round. Seven under for the tournament.

We walked off the green soaked to the bone but charged with adrenaline. He was tied for second, right in the hunt. I was buzzing, feeling like we had a real shot at winning it all.

John saw the excitement in my eyes and placed a hand on my shoulder. "Stay focused, Mac," he said. "And make sure I do the same."

Day 3 – Moving Day

Golfers call the third round "Moving Day" because it's where contenders separate from the pack. John knew it, and so did Ken Rodewald. They had made a side bet—$100 on who would shoot the better round.

At the turn, John was already four under for the day. He was locked in, and we were working like a well-oiled machine. I handed him clubs before he even asked for them. We read the greens together, our instincts in sync.

On the back nine, he caught fire. Birdie at 12. Another at 14. A tricky up-and-down for par at 16 kept the momentum alive. When he sank a curling 10-footer for birdie on 18, he pumped his fist.

Final score: 14 under for the tournament. Tied for the lead.

Ken had matched him stroke for stroke, so their side bet came down to a single shot. John had edged him by one. As we walked to the scoring tent, John slipped a crisp ten-dollar bill into my palm.

"Mac," he said, "You've earned this."

I smirked. "I told you I'd do it for five."

He grinned. "Consider it a tip."

Final Round – The Heartbreaker

The rain had softened the greens, making them more receptive, but the wind was brutal. Flags whipped in the gusts, and every tee shot felt like a gamble.

John came out firing. Birdies on 2, 4, 6, and 9 put him at 19 under. He had the lead.

Then came the 10th hole.

A wayward drive into the deep rough. An awkward lie. A forced punch-out that landed short. A missed par putt.

A bogey.

Then another on 11. And another on 12.

Golf is cruel. Momentum is fragile. One mistake can lead to another, and before you know it, the game has slipped through your fingers.

John fought back, but Ken was relentless. A birdie on 17 sealed it. John needed an eagle on 18 to tie, but his second shot landed just short of the green. The chip ran past the hole, and his birdie putt lipped out.

Ken Rodewald won at 20 under. John finished second at 19.

The Aftermath

The locker room was quiet.

John sat on a bench, staring at the floor, his hands clasped together. The room smelled of damp towels, sweat, and the faint scent of disappointment. I stood near the doorway, unsure of what to say.

"John, I'm sorry I let you down," I said.

He looked up, his expression unreadable at first. Then, he shook his head and let out a quiet chuckle.

"Mac, you didn't let me down. I let a couple of bad shots get to me." He reached into his pocket and handed me a five-dollar bill. "You did great this week."

I took it, but it didn't feel like a victory.

As I left the locker room, I spotted Ken leaning against the wall outside, waiting for me. He folded his arms and gave me an appraising look.

"Mac," he said, "You're a natural caddie. I know some folks at Orchard Ridge and Fort Wayne Country Club who'd love to have someone like you. Interested?"

I hesitated. "I'd have to ask me mum and dad."

Ken nodded. "Let me know. You've got a bright future, kid."

As I walked home, I felt two things at once—pride and sadness.

Pride because I had proven myself. I wasn't just some kid carrying clubs. I was part of the game, part of something bigger than myself.

But sadness, too. Because I had wanted this win for John. I had wanted to see him hoist that trophy, to celebrate together. I had learned something important that day.

Golf, like life, doesn't always give you the fairytale ending.

But it does give you the chance to get back up.

CHAPTER 3

Wheels

Walking home, I couldn't stop thinking about what Ken had said. Caddying at Orchard Ridge or Fort Wayne Country Club would be a big step up—Mom would call them *posh*. The word fit. Rumors among the caddies said the pay was double what we made at Foster Park—two dollars a loop instead of one.

I did some quick math in my head. If I could work both courses on the weekends, I might manage three loops a day—twelve dollars a weekend. That was real money. But there was a problem—both clubs were three miles away.

Mom and Dad would insist my grades not suffer, but I knew I could handle it. I just needed a way to get there.

As I rounded the corner by the hardware store, something in the window made me stop—a Schwinn Corvette.

It was the latest and greatest in bicycles—sleek, royal blue, with chrome fenders that gleamed under the store lights. The curved handlebars, white-wall tires, and three-speed gear shift made it look like it could fly.

I stepped inside, unable to resist a closer look.

"Don't get your hopes up too high, Gavin," said Pete, the store manager, grinning as he wiped his hands on a rag. "That's a mighty fine bike, but it ain't cheap."

"How much?" I asked, already bracing for disappointment.

"Thirty dollars."

I exhaled and ran a hand along the smooth frame. "Someday," I murmured.

A Plan in Motion

At home, Mom had a sandwich waiting for me. "How'd the tournament go?" she asked, setting a glass of milk in front of me.

"John finished second," I said between bites.

Mom clapped her hands. "That's wonderful!"

I shook my head. "Would've been a lot more wonderful if he'd won." But then I smiled. "Good news is, John thought I did a great job. Even better—the winner, Ken Rodewald, said he could help me get on as a caddie at Orchard Ridge and maybe even Fort Wayne Country Club!"

Mom beamed. "We're so proud of you! But you'll have to talk to your father first."

"I know." I sighed and finished my sandwich, already running through how I'd present my case to Dad.

He got home around five, and I figured I'd wait a bit—let him have his usual dram of Scotch before bringing it up. But before I could, there was a knock on my door.

Dad stepped in. "You and John gave it a good go this week." He folded his arms. "I hope he paid you your five dollars."

I grinned and pulled out the bills. "He did—and even extra!"

Dad raised an eyebrow. "My, my. That's a lot of money for a young lad."

"Don't worry," I said with a wink. "I'm a Scotsman through and through."

He chuckled. "That's my boy. I'll take you to the bank in the morning."

"Well…" I hesitated. "I was thinking of investing it."

Dad scoffed. "What in the name of our good Lord do you know about investing?"

I explained about the tips at the country clubs and how I could make twice as much caddying there. "Lawyers and doctor types, you know. I figure I could make twelve dollars a weekend—maybe more if they tip."

Dad frowned. "I've no problem with a young man wanting to work. But those clubs are three miles away."

"I know, but—"

"But nothing," he interrupted. "You can't be walking six miles a day on top of carrying bags."

I pulled out the flyer Pete had given me. "I have almost half the money now. I could earn the rest in two weekends—or maybe the bank would loan me the rest, and I'd pay it off over time."

Dad sighed. "You're not old enough for a loan." Then, after a long pause, he added, "And even if you were, I'd tell you to put that money toward college—or better yet, a trade school."

He turned and left, slamming the door behind him.

But instead of discouraging me, his reaction only made me more determined.

The Deal

At supper, the silence was heavy. I finished eating and excused myself, but Dad stopped me.

"Get back here and sit down. I'm not done with you."

I sat.

He sighed, glancing at Mom. "Your mother and I talked it over. Here's what's going to happen. If you promise to keep your grades at a B average, we'll loan you the rest. You'll pay us a dollar a week while you're working, and you'll do any chores we ask during the winter."

I stuck out my hand. "Deal!"

The next day, I became the proud owner of a royal blue 1957 Schwinn Corvette.

As we left the store, I grinned at Dad. "Thanks! See ya later!"

"Where are you going, boy?" he called.

"To Foster Park to find Ken and John!" I yelled, already pedaling away.

Ken was just pulling into the parking lot when I arrived.

"Nice bike, Mac."

I puffed out my chest. "Got it so I can get to the other clubs you told me about."

"Good for you," he said. "When can you start?"

"This weekend."

"Great. I'll call the pros and give them your name."

Orchard Ridge & FWCC

I rode straight to Orchard Ridge, eager to see what awaited me. The place was stunning—rolling fairways, manicured greens, and towering trees. It felt like stepping onto sacred ground.

Inside the pro shop, a stern-looking man eyed me.

"Can I help you, young man?"

"I'm looking for the pro."

"That'd be me," he said, shaking my hand. "Name's Jon Sevajas. And you are?"

"Mac…Ken Rodewald called about me."

His expression softened. "Hoping to walk the course?"

"Aye."

He showed me around, pointing out the tricky holes and subtle slopes. At the end, he handed me a leather-bound yardage book.

"I caddied here for three years. This was mine. Study it, but don't lose it."

I held it like a relic. "I won't lie…be careful out there," he told me. "I have got a few hackers out there today."

I headed up the first fairway, checking yardages and looking at Jon's caddie book. I wandered into the rough to get a feel for what kind of trouble an errant shot might bring. Suddenly, a ball came flying at me and whizzed right by my nose.

A couple of minutes later, this guy comes up and says, "My God, boy, where did you come from?"

I told him I was going to be a caddie and was just getting the lay of the land.

"Well, did you see where my ball landed?" he asked.

"Not really, but it got close enough. I knew it was a Titleist 2."

He chuckled and said, "I'm sorry, young man. What's your name?"

"Mac," I replied.

He stuck out his hand and said, "Folks call me Doc Willy."

"Nice to meet you, Doc," I replied.

We found his ball buried in the rough.

"Oh, brother. Now what?" he exclaimed.

I told him to take a wedge and punch it out to the fairway.

I continued, "You'll still be out about 166, but the green is pretty big. If you get on and make your putt, you still get par!"

He gave me a look, shrugged his shoulders, and said, "Here goes nothin."

He hit it well and got it back out in the middle of the fairway.

I looked in the book Jon gave me and said, "Doc, it's 165 to the pin from right here. According to the book, the green slopes left to right. There's some wind up there, so give it all you got and aim to land it pin-high, left edge of the green."

He hit it and said, "Well, I'll be. You're pretty good at this stuff."

"Doc, I'm just getting started."

I walked a few more holes with him, and we got along great. Doc said, "Mac, next time I play, I'd like to hire you as my caddie."

I said that would be an honor. It started a friendship that lasted for years.

First Day at FWCC

Fort Wayne Country Club was even grander. I had walked this course before, but now, I had gotten a chance to work here. The clubhouse looked like something from a movie, the fairways pristine.

I checked in and found the caddie bench. The older boys looked me over.

"How you gonna carry clubs with arms that small?" one sneered.

"He's so short, the bag's gonna drag," another snickered.

Before I could respond, a tall, older caddie stepped forward.

"Name's Gerry…with a G," he said, shaking my hand. "You're the kid who caddied for John in the city tournament?"

"That'd be me."

He turned to the others. "Listen up. This is Mac. He caddied for the second-place finisher. Show him some respect."

The others straightened.

"Yes, sir," they said in unison.

I grinned.

Just then, a voice crackled over the megaphone.

"Next on the tee, the Rodewald group. McTavish, Whitten, you're up."

Kenny smiled at me. "Good to see ya, Mac. My bag's second from the end. Grab it and meet me on the tee box."

I wiped his driver and handed it over. He pulled a caddie book from his pocket and tossed it to me.

"You'll need this."

I looked at him, stunned. "Thanks, Mr. Ro—"

"Call me Kenny," he said. "Or I'll call you Mr. McTavish for the rest of your life."

I laughed.

By the time I pedaled home that night—exhausted but exhilarated—I knew this was just the beginning.

CHAPTER 4

A Gentleman and a Scholar (Part 1)

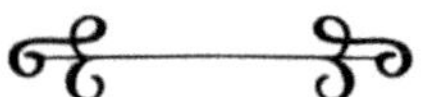

For the next two years, I caddied regularly at both country clubs. The long hours and heavy bags didn't bother me much. I paid off my debt to my parents quickly and even started saving for my first automobile.

By the end of the summer, I caddied nearly seventy rounds, and I wasn't shy about bragging it to Kenny.

"Seventy rounds, huh?" he said one afternoon, adjusting his cap against the sun.

"That's right," I replied with pride.

Kenny smirked. "How're your grades?"

"Solid B-plus," I said.

"Good," he said, nodding. "Come with me. I've got something for you."

Curious, I followed him to his car. He leaned inside and pulled out an envelope with my name on it. Handing it to me, he said, "It's a little something for your future."

I stared at the return address: **Evans Scholars Foundation.**

"What is this?" I asked, the words barely audible.

"It's a great shot at a full ride to Indiana University," Kenny said with a grin. "Take it home and go over it with your mom and dad."

That evening at dinner, I slid the envelope across the table to my parents.

"What's this?" Dad asked, squinting at the writing.

"It's a scholarship opportunity," I said, my excitement bubbling over. "The Evans Scholarship. It's a full tuition and housing scholarship for caddies! They've been doing this since 1930, helping kids like me get to college."

Mom's smile lit up the room. "That's incredible, Gavin!"

Dad raised an eyebrow. "What does it take to get it?"

I opened the packet and explained. The first section verified the rounds I'd caddied—a total of 67—signed by both club pros.

The next section focused on financial hardship. I noticed Dad shift uncomfortably.

"I can fill this out," Mom said gently, sensing his hesitation. "Gavin, you'll need to complete the personal essays."

"I will," I promised.

For the next two days, I poured my heart into those essays, writing about what caddying had taught me—hard work, responsibility, perseverance. When I handed them to Mom, she gave me a reassuring nod.

"I'll send it off by registered mail tomorrow," she said.

And then, the waiting began.

In the weeks that followed, I threw myself into my schoolwork like never before. I was determined to make straight A's, and for the first time, I felt like it was within my reach.

When my final report card arrived, I handed it to Mom with a grin.

"A perfect 4.0!" she exclaimed.

Dad, however, had been unusually quiet. One evening, I found him staring out at the flower garden, his hands in his pockets.

"Hey, Dad," I said, stepping outside. "What's on your mind?"

He sighed, his shoulders heavy. "You've always had us close by, Gavin. Now you're heading off on your own. It scares me, son. People out there will try to take advantage of you."

"Dad," I said, placing a hand on his shoulder, "You've taught me everything I need to know. I feel ready. I feel like I've earned this."

For a moment, he didn't say anything. Then he nodded, a flicker of pride in his eyes.

"You're gonna do great things, son."

The letter came the next day. I had, in fact, been selected as an Evans Scholarship recipient. The letter thoroughly explained the benefits and the duties I would have in return.

CHAPTER 4

The Evans House (Part 2)

The Evans Scholarship House loomed before me—a stately brick building nestled within the sprawling Indiana University campus. Its wide front steps led to a welcoming entryway, and the sound of laughter spilling from the windows made it feel both intimidating and inviting.

I hoisted my suitcase and stepped inside. A group of young men gathered in the common room paused their chatter, turning to look at me.

"New guy?" one of them asked—a tall junior with an easy smile.

"Aye, Gavin McAlister," I replied, my Scottish accent drawing a few raised eyebrows and smirks.

"Well, Gavin, welcome to the House," he said, shaking my hand. "I'm Tim. You'll find the chore list on the board in the kitchen. And don't forget—study hall is mandatory every weeknight."

"Most people call me Mac," I added.

The Evans House ran like a well-oiled machine. Chores and study hours weren't suggestions—they were expectations. But within the structure, there was an unspoken bond. These young men weren't just housemates; they were brothers, bound by shared struggles and ambitions.

I knew I'd have to find a job soon—the scholarship covered tuition, books, and housing, but food and other expenses were on me.

It was as if I had stepped into an entirely new world. Gone were the comforts of home, replaced by the unfamiliar sights and sounds of fraternity life. The hierarchy unfolded before my eyes—upperclassmen strutting around like roosters in a henhouse, while freshmen scrambled to prove themselves. I wondered where I would fit into this pecking order, but I had no doubt I'd find my place.

And then there was the reality of being away from home for the first time. I had never spent a night outside my parents' house before. Now, here I was, at the university, responsible for myself.

It was exhilarating.

A Hustle for Every Dollar

Money was tight. After a week of scouring campus bulletin boards and asking around, I landed a job at the university dining hall—serving meals, wiping down tables, and washing dishes.

My first shift was chaos. Students poured in nonstop, trays piled high, and my supervisor barked orders like a drill sergeant. My arms ached from scrubbing industrial-sized pots, but I gritted my teeth and worked through it. By the end of the night, I was exhausted—but proud.

Balancing school, work, and responsibilities at the Evans House wasn't easy. Late at night, I pored over textbooks under the dim glow of my desk lamp, fighting off fatigue. But I thrived on the challenge, knowing every dish I washed brought me closer to my dreams.

I also caddied whenever I could—not just for the money, but for the free golf. It was my escape, my way of staying connected to the game I loved.

Emma

It was a Friday evening when I first saw her.

After my shift at the dining hall, I stopped by the student union for a coffee. She sat at a nearby table, her auburn hair catching the light as she laughed with a friend.

As I passed, she glanced up and smiled—a fleeting moment that stopped me in my tracks.

"Do you always stare, or am I just lucky?" she teased, her blue eyes full of amusement.

Blushing, I stammered, "I didn't mean to—sorry, I just—"

She laughed again, setting me at ease. "I'm Emma. And you are?"

"Gavin. Gavin McAlister."

From that moment, conversation flowed effortlessly. Emma was studying English, dreaming of becoming a teacher, and her passion for literature captivated me. Over the weeks, we grew closer—meeting for walks around campus, sharing late-night talks over coffee.

Our relationship wasn't without challenges. My packed schedule left little time for Emma, and at times, she grew frustrated with my tendency to put work and school above all else. But we always found our way back to each other, our bond strengthening with every hurdle.

One crisp autumn evening, we sat on a bench overlooking campus, fallen leaves crunching underfoot as students passed by, their laughter and chatter fading into the background.

"Do you ever think about what's next?" Emma asked, breaking the comfortable silence.

"All the time."

Mad Anthony and the St. John's Mafia

Over the summer break, I headed home to Fort Wayne and to the comfort of my old bed in order to spend time with mom and dad. Summers in Fort Wayne had always meant one thing—golf. Between rounds at Foster Park and caddying at the country clubs, I had built a reputation as a reliable, knowledgeable looper. But the highlight of summers was always the Mad Anthony's Pro-Am, an event that brought professional golfers, local amateurs, and a whole cast of characters together for a weekend of competition, camaraderie, and a fair share of chaos.

This year, I found myself in the mix once again. The tournament was a blend of serious golf and lighthearted antics, where elite players shared fairways with local legends and businessmen who had more money than skill. All in the name of charity.

Mad Anthony's was a break for me as a looper. No lugging bags—just playing the game I loved. My favorite foursome had a reputation as the most entertaining group in the field. They called themselves the "St. John's Mafia"—a tight-knit crew of Catholic guys who had grown up together, played in every local tournament, and made it their mission to have more fun on the course than anyone else. They were excellent golfers, but their real talent was in pranks and good-natured ribbing.

I got paired up with Big Eddie, a burly guy with a cigar permanently wedged in the corner of his mouth.

"Hope you've got thick skin," he said.

I'd barely slung my bag over my shoulder before I felt a hard slap on the back.

"Hey, you're that kid from Foster who won that caddie scholarship, right? You ever play with a saint before?" asked Jimmy O'Brien, a wiry Irishman with a wicked grin.

"Can't say I have," I replied.

"Good, because there ain't a saint in the group," Jimmy shot back, sending the group into a fit of laughter.

As the round unfolded, the Mafia kept up their antics. They placed bets on who could sink the longest putt using the wrong end of the putter. They faked arguments over meaningless rules and forced me to "mediate." At one point, Big Eddie pretended to throw his wedge into a water hazard, only to reveal he had a second one hidden in his bag.

The group's ringleader, Paulie Delvecchio, was notorious for his annual prank at the tournament. This year, he had arranged for a friend dressed as a Catholic priest to show up on the 9th green, sprinkling "holy water" (which smelled a lot like whiskey) onto his putter for divine intervention.

"Father, give this club your blessing," Paulie intoned solemnly.

The "priest" complied, and Paulie drained a 40-footer, sending the entire green into an uproar.

While Mad Anthony's was all about fun, the pro-ams at the country clubs were more serious. I'd looped for a few different professionals, each with their own unique quirks.

I remember one player insisting I stand perfectly still and toss blades of grass into the air before every shot—even on the green. Another had a superstition that required me to always hand him his 7-iron first, no matter what club he actually needed.

Then there was Tommy "Two Gloves" Reynolds, a journeyman pro who, true to his nickname, wore two gloves on every shot—even when putting. Tommy had a habit of talking through every shot, often asking me for advice only to do the exact opposite.

"You sure this is an 8-iron, kid?" he'd ask, eyeing the distance.

"Yes, sir. 150 yards, slight wind in," I replied.

"Yeah… nah, I'm going with a soft 6," Tommy would say, before promptly blasting the ball over the green.

After a time or two, I figured out the key to keeping the pros happy—stay confident, offer advice when asked, and never, ever laugh when they messed up.

On the final day of my summer vacation, I had plans to loop at Sycamore Hills. I was paired with a pro named Jack Callahan. Unlike some of the others, Callahan was all business. He played a smooth, disciplined game, and I quickly earned his respect by reading greens and keeping the bag light.

As we walked up the 18th fairway, Callahan turned to me.

"You ever think about caddying full-time?" he asked.

I was caught off guard. "I mean, sure, but I'm still in school."

Callahan nodded. "You've got a good feel for the game. You keep your cool. That's rare. I could use a guy like you on tour."

My heart pounded. A full-time job as a caddie on the pro tour? It was a dream I hadn't even allowed myself to consider.

"I don't need an answer today," Callahan said. "But think about it. I'll be in touch."

That night, I sat on the porch, staring out at the quiet Fort Wayne streets. The offer was everything I could have wanted—traveling the country, working with the best golfers in the world, making a name for myself.

But then there was Emma.

We had spent so much time together over the school semester, growing closer with every round of golf, every late-night talk, every moment stolen in between my caddie gigs. She had dreams of her own, and she had always supported me. But this…this was different. This was a life that might take me away from her.

I picked up the phone, dialing her number with shaky hands.

"Hey, Mac," she said, her voice warm and familiar.

"Hey," I replied, taking a deep breath. "I've got something to tell you."

Life Swing

In my final year at IU, I signed up to caddie at Crooked Stick for their pro-am. I'd spent years walking the fairways—first as a wide-eyed boy learning the game, then as a young man honing my craft as a caddie. But the pro-am tournament at Crooked Stick felt different. The air carried a certain electricity, the locker room chatter had an edge of seriousness, and the players—both amateurs and professionals—moved with a quiet intensity that told me I was stepping into a new world.

I had been assigned to an insurance executive from Chicago, a weekend warrior with more enthusiasm than skill. I enjoyed the banter and gave the best advice I could, but my attention kept drifting to the professionals playing alongside us. These men weren't just playing the game; they were living it.

And then I saw him—Jack Callahan.

He's the guy I met at the Sycamore Hills Pro Am. He was one of the young guns on tour, known for his precision and steady nerves. Unlike some of the other pros who merely tolerated the amateurs for the sake of the tournament, Jack was patient and engaged, coaching his partner through every hole. He carried himself with quiet confidence, but I could see the fire beneath the surface.

By the back nine, I had stopped watching my own player's errant shots and started studying Jack's game—his approach to each hole, the way he calculated risk, the trust he placed in his caddie. Jack's bagman was an older guy who seemed to be struggling with the long walk. By the 16th hole, the man was lagging behind, rubbing his knee and wincing.

After Jack tapped in for par, he turned to me.

"Hey, kid," he said, his voice smooth and measured. "You ever consider working with a pro?"

I blinked, caught off guard. "I'd be lying if I said the thought never crossed my mind."

Jack nodded, as if he already knew the answer. "My guy's retiring after this season. I need someone sharp, someone who knows the game beyond just carrying a bag. You interested?"

I hesitated. The words *interested?* and *dream job* felt synonymous in my mind. But then Emma's face flashed before me, and my stomach twisted.

"I…have thought about it, but I've still got another semester before I graduate. I need to look at the income potential… and my marriage."

Jack smiled. "Good answer. Smart not to jump at the first offer. But I'll tell you this—you've got the instincts. I saw you reading putts for your guy today. You knew the breaks before he even lined up. And you carry yourself well."

CHAPTER 5

A Future in Motion

The final semester at Indiana University passed in a blur—exams, late-night study sessions, and a carefully balanced mix of responsibilities. By now, I had grown accustomed to the rhythm of it all: shifts at the dining hall, time with Emma, long hours in the Evans House study room, and the occasional round of golf when I could spare an afternoon.

As graduation loomed, so did the weight of the real world. The uncertainty of what came next gnawed at me. During my last semester, I took an elective course in business communication—a decision that would prove pivotal. The professor, a sharp-tongued but insightful mentor, took notice of me.

"You've got the gift of persuasion, McAlister," he said after my presentation on the art of networking. "Don't waste it."

I didn't.

Instead, I poured my energy into job applications, focusing on companies connected to my passion for golf. Among them was Titleist—a name that had always carried weight in my mind since my early days as a caddie.

Graduation and a Gift to Remember

May arrived with blooming flowers and a profound sense of accomplishment. I was graduating. My parents traveled from Fort Wayne to celebrate, their pride evident in the way my mother kept dabbing her eyes and the way my father clapped me on the back a little harder than necessary. Emma stood beside them, beaming as I crossed the stage to accept my diploma.

After the ceremony, we gathered for a quiet dinner. As we finished our meal, my father reached into his pocket and handed me a small box. I opened it to find a tie clip in the shape of a golf club.

"It's not much," he said, his voice thick with emotion. "But it's a reminder of where you started—and how far you've come."

I swallowed the lump in my throat, turning the tie clip over in my hand. "Thanks, Dad. I couldn't have done this without you and Mom."

A Foot in the Door

A few weeks after graduation, I got the news I had been hoping for—Titleist wanted me to join their sales team. It was an entry-level internship, but it was exactly the foot in the door I needed.

Excitement and nerves battled inside me as I walked into the office for my first day. It was a whirlwind of introductions, training sessions, and stacks of product manuals. But I quickly found my stride. My background in golf gave me an edge—I didn't just know the equipment, I understood the players, their frustrations, their needs, and their dreams.

"You've got the magic," my supervisor joked one day after I closed a particularly difficult sale. Then he raised an eyebrow and asked, "How do you feel about travel, Mac?"

A New Chapter with Emma

By this time, my relationship with Emma had deepened. We spent countless evenings dreaming about our future—she longed to teach in a small town, and I envisioned a life traveling for work but always returning home to her.

One warm summer evening, while visiting my parents in Fort Wayne, I proposed. We were walking along the familiar fairways of Foster Park Golf Course—the same course where I had spent so many summers caddying. As the sun dipped below the horizon, I knelt down and, with my heart pounding, asked Emma to be my wife.

Through happy tears, she said yes.

Our wedding was a modest affair, held at the local church with family, friends, and a few of my colleagues from Titleist in attendance. My father gave a heartfelt toast at the reception, my mother cried happy tears, and Emma looked radiant—her joy lighting up the room.

Two Decades on the Fairway

The next twenty years passed in a blur. My career at Titleist had taken me all over the country, from private clubs tucked away in the Carolina mountains to sprawling resorts in Arizona and California. I was good at my job—not just because I knew the game, but because I understood the people who played it. I could walk into a pro shop and talk to a club pro like we'd been friends for years. I knew how to read a customer, when to push a sale, and when to step back and let the clubs do the talking.

It was a good life. A fulfilling one. Emma and I built a home in Indiana, raised two kids, and made a life that felt solid and steady. Through all the travel, all the business dinners and tournaments, she was my constant. She understood the rhythm of my work, the way golf had always been in my blood.

One evening, we sat on the porch watching the sunset, the sky painted in warm hues of orange and gold. I swirled the last sip of my drink in my glass and exhaled.

"You know," I said, staring out at the yard, "I've been thinking about retiring someday. Maybe even going back to Foster Park Golf Course. Working in the pro shop, helping kids learn the game."

Emma smiled, her hands folded over her lap. "That sounds perfect."

I nodded, lost in thought. From the windswept courses of my childhood in Scotland to the rolling fairways of Indiana, my life had been built around this game. But for the first time, I felt the pull of something else—the need to come home.

A Life-Altering Phone Call

The thought of returning to Foster Park stayed with me, creeping into my mind at odd hours—on long flights, in hotel rooms, even in the middle of a sales meeting. Then, one afternoon, my phone rang. It was my mother.

Her voice was shaky. "Your father had a heart attack today, Mac. Out on the course… mowing the greens."

I gripped the phone. "Is he—?"

She inhaled sharply. "He's gone."

Gone. Just like that.

Emma came into the room and took one look at my face before wrapping me in a tight embrace.

"He knew you were coming home," she whispered. "It's almost like he was waiting for you to take over."

I nodded, but the guilt was already sinking in. I hadn't been there. He had been my hero—my teacher, my friend. And I wasn't there when it mattered most.

That night, memories flooded my mind. I thought of him teaching me how to ride a bike, how to mow fairways in those perfect, even lines. I remembered the way he'd explain things in that patient, deliberate way of his—the right way to hold a club, the importance of respect on the course, how to carry yourself, not just as a golfer, but as a man.

I should have been there.

As I packed for the trip home, Emma found something tucked away in an old box—my Evans Scholarship acceptance letter. She handed it to me, her eyes full of understanding.

"This started it all," I said quietly, running my fingers over the worn edges of the paper.

She smiled. "And now you're closing the loop."

The Funeral & The Pull of Home

The funeral was a blur of familiar faces and hushed voices. People I hadn't seen in decades shook my hand, clapped me on the shoulder, and shared their own stories of my father.

As I sat in the church, surrounded by friends, family, and old caddies who had once walked the same fairways as me, I realized something. My father's legacy wasn't just in the grass he cut or the holes he kept pristine. It was in the people whose lives he had touched.

And that's when I knew. It was time to go home.

Foster Park Had Changed

Returning to Foster Park Golf Course was like stepping into a memory that had been stretched and reshaped by time.

Some things were familiar—the scent of fresh-cut grass, the way the early morning sun glowed over the fairways. But other things had changed.

The Fort Wayne Parks and Recreation Department had decided that having a golf professional manage merchandise, carts, and concessions was unnecessary. Instead, those responsibilities had been shuffled off to other departments, leaving the course without the leadership it once had.

I heard grumblings from the regulars, who missed having a pro in the shop—someone who understood the game, not just the bottom line. Foster Park was the oldest of the four public courses in Fort Wayne—Shoaff, McMillen, Mad Anthony, and this one. It had history. Tradition. And yet, decisions were being made by people who had never spent a day walking these fairways.

I made it my mission to change that.

First Day Back at the Pro Shop

Walking into the pro shop on my first day, I felt the weight of both nostalgia and responsibility. The place smelled the same—leather, sunblock, and fresh scorecards. The counters were lined with neatly folded polo shirts, and the register still made that satisfying ding when it popped open.

And then, I saw him.

Standing at the counter, leaning slightly forward, squinting at the screen, was a man I had known since my first days as a caddy.

"John?" I said, my voice catching.

He turned slowly, adjusting the thick magnifying glass in his hand, and then his face broke into a grin. "Mac? No. It can't be."

I walked over, shaking my head with a chuckle. "You still working here after all these years?"

John laughed. "Somebody's gotta keep this place running."

But as I watched him fumble with the register, struggling to see the screen, I realized just how much time had taken its toll.

After Rick, the supervisor, pulled me aside. "John won't admit it, but his eyesight's gotten worse. He walks to work every morning, rain or shine because he can't drive anymore."

That didn't sit right with me.

The next morning, I pulled up in front of John's house at 6:45 a.m.

When he opened the door, his face twisted in confusion. "What are you doing here?"

I smiled. "Giving you a ride."

From that day forward, it became our routine.

Standing on the porch with Emma that night, looking out at the same sky we had watched decades before, I finally felt at peace.

Coming back to Foster Park wasn't just about me.

It was about giving back. About honoring the past while shaping the future.

And in that moment, I knew—I had finally come home.

CHAPTER 6

The First Student

My first student was a shy kid—slightly autistic but sharp as a tack. His name was Pete. He was in high school, quiet but observant, with a mind that worked faster than most. His dad reached out, saying Pete had an interest in golf but had never taken lessons. He thought I might be a good fit.

We met for the first time at his dad's house. Pete sat across from me, shifting in his seat, his fingers tracing patterns along the grain of the table. I decided to ease into it.

"What's your favorite subject in school?" I asked.

"Math," he said without hesitation.

I grinned. "That's fantastic! Golf is all about math."

Pete let out a small chuckle, his voice edged with skepticism. "You mean like adding up your score?"

"Well, there's that," I said, smirking. "But golf is a lot more complex than just keeping score. Distance to the hole changes with every shot. The club you choose is critical, and knowing how far you can hit each club is absolutely necessary."

He muttered a thoughtful "Hmm."

"Oh, that's just the beginning, Pete," I said, leaning forward. "Wait until we get to the geometry."

"Geometry?" His eyebrow lifted.

"Sure," I said. "And even a little calculus."

His curiosity piqued. "I had no idea. I thought golf was just about hitting the ball as far as you can."

"Yeah," I said with a knowing smile. "A lot of people think that."

We scheduled our first lesson for the following Wednesday.

Pete's dad hesitated. "How long do you expect a lesson to last?"

"Just over an hour," I said.

His dad exhaled. "Pete has never spent that much time with an adult he doesn't know."

I smiled. "Well, I accept that challenge."

Breaking Through

That Wednesday morning, I was already at the course when I saw Pete and his dad walking up the path. Pete's hands were shoved deep into his pockets, his gaze flicking between the clubhouse and the putting green.

"We're going to start with putting," I told him. "The goal is simple—get the ball in the hole in as few strokes as possible. But here's where the math comes in: you have to calculate distance, whether the green slopes uphill or downhill, and if the ball will break left or right."

Pete nodded, taking it in.

"This shot here is about two feet," I continued. "It's uphill. Give it a try."

His first putt stopped halfway there. His second raced past the hole by six feet.

He sighed in frustration.

"That's why we're here," I said. "You're learning. It's all about touch and feel."

We spent the rest of the hour working on pace and reading the green. He was hesitant at first, second-guessing every stroke, but by the end of the lesson, I could see a shift—he was thinking, analyzing, beginning to understand the game in a way that most beginners didn't.

The Moment It Clicked

Over the summer, we met twice a week. We focused on putting and chipping first—because that's where most strokes happen. Pete was a natural with the numbers.

One day, I wanted to challenge him. "Alright, Pete," I said. "I want you to walk uphill to the hole and count your steps. Then, start at the right edge of the green and walk the steps from there to the back of the hole."

Pete did as I asked, then turned back to me, his finger tapping his lip as he worked through the calculations in his head.

"Two feet and four and a half inches," he said. "From right to left."

I stared at him, stunned. It had taken me years to develop an eye for that kind of precision. Pete had figured it out in minutes.

"I think you're right," I said, stepping back. "Now putt it."

He lined up, took a steady breath, and stroked the ball.

We both watched in silence as it rolled, broke exactly as he predicted, and dropped straight into the cup.

For a moment, neither of us said a word. Then Pete's face lit up with a grin so wide it could have split the sky.

His excitement was contagious. My chest swelled with pride—not just because he made the putt, but because, right then, I saw that he believed in himself.

When I walked him to his dad's car, I told him, "The next few lessons, we'll be playing the course. That means we'll need about two hours."

Pete's dad hesitated, frowning. "Two hours?"

Before I could respond, Pete blurted out, "Please let me do this!"

His dad's expression softened, and he gave a small nod.

The Golfer Pete Became

For the last two weeks of summer, we played four nine-hole rounds. I acted as his caddie—helping him with club selection, gauging wind speed, and, more than anything, building his confidence.

On our final round together, Pete made two legitimate birdies. He ran to his dad's car afterward, practically bouncing. "Dad! Did you see that? Two birdies!"

His dad ruffled his hair, pride clear in his eyes.

Even after our lessons ended, Pete and his dad kept showing up every weekend. Golf had become part of him.

A year later, Pete went off to Purdue on a golf scholarship, studying engineering. I'd see him in the summers when he was home, and each time, he was better than before.

Then, one day, I heard the news—Pete had won the Big Ten Tournament.

I let out a long whistle when I read it. I had taught dozens of students over the years—some had talent, some had passion, and some had both. But none of them had been quite like Pete.

He was the first student I ever had. And the one I'd never forget.

He went on to become a PGA touring pro.

Chapter 7

The Supervisor

Foster Park Golf Course had always felt like home, but stepping into the role of supervisor changed everything. I wasn't just teaching golf anymore—I was managing people, ensuring the course ran smoothly, and training my staff to provide top-notch service.

The team was a mixed bag: ten employees, including myself and John. Most were retired men looking for something to do with their mornings, two retired women who brought a much-needed balance to the group, and one younger guy working his second job. Each had their quirks, their habits, and their own way of doing things. My job was to make sure they all worked toward the same goal—increasing sales, improving customer service, and keeping the course running like a well-oiled machine.

The Sleeper

It didn't take long before I ran into my first problem.

One afternoon, I walked the cart path near the maintenance shed and spotted a golf cart parked in the shade of a tree. At first, I thought nothing of it. But as I got closer, I saw someone slumped back in the seat, hat pulled over his face, arms folded across his chest.

Sleeping.

I sighed.

The man in question was Jerry—one of the older guys, known for his easygoing nature. Too easygoing, it seemed. I tapped the side of the cart lightly, and Jerry jolted awake, adjusting his hat and clearing his throat.

"Everything alright, Jerry?" I asked, keeping my tone light but firm.

He rubbed his eyes. "Oh yeah, just taking a little break."

I crossed my arms. "A little break, huh?"

He chuckled. "You know how it is, Mac. These early shifts catch up with you."

I nodded. "I get it. But here's the thing—we're not getting paid to nap. The customers expect us to be alert and available. If they see an employee sleeping in a cart, what do you think they're gonna think?"

Jerry scratched his head. "That we don't care?"

"Exactly," I said. "And I know that's not true. You've been around here long enough to know how much this course means to the regulars. They count on us."

Jerry sighed and sat up straighter. "Alright, alright. No more snoozing."

I clapped him on the shoulder. "Appreciate it, Jerry. Now, how about we make sure all the carts are stocked and lined up for the afternoon rush?"

He nodded, a little embarrassed but understanding.

That was the thing about managing people—you couldn't just lay down the law. You had to make them see why it mattered.

The Stubborn One

Another challenge came in the form of Ed. Ed was one of the most well-intentioned guys on staff, but he had a habit of messing up his daily reports. Every time he worked the register, there was a discrepancy—cash missing, sales miscounted, or tee times booked incorrectly.

At first, I thought it was a simple mistake, but after the third time, I knew I had to address it.

"Ed," I said one morning as I sat beside him in the pro shop, reviewing the previous day's report. "Looks like we're off by twenty dollars again."

He frowned. "Well, it wasn't me."

I exhaled slowly. "Okay, but you were the only one on shift at the time."

He shook his head. "I count the drawer just like I'm supposed to."

I could tell he was getting defensive. This was the tricky part. I had to correct him without making him feel like I was accusing him of stealing.

"Look, Ed, I know you're doing your best," I said. "But these mistakes keep happening, and I need to figure out why. Let's walk through your process together."

He huffed but followed along as I had him step through his routine.

Sure enough, within minutes, we found the issue—he was entering cash transactions twice and then removing one, throwing off the balance.

Ed sighed, rubbing his temple. "Guess I've been doing it wrong this whole time."

I smiled. "It's an easy fix. Let's run through it again, just to make sure we've got it right."

We went over the system until he was comfortable. I could tell he was relieved.

"You know," he said as he logged out of the register, "I appreciate you not jumping down my throat about this."

I shrugged. "We're all here to make the course better. No sense in making it harder than it needs to be."

He nodded. "I'll be more careful."

The Bigger Picture

Running Foster Park wasn't just about keeping the fairways in shape or making sure the carts were charged; it was about the people—the customers who showed up every morning, the kids who came for lessons, and the staff who kept everything running.

I was learning that managing wasn't so different from teaching golf. It wasn't just about knowing the rules; it was about understanding people and knowing when to push and when to encourage.

And just like on the course, sometimes the smallest adjustments made the biggest difference.

Chapter 8

The Deep Rough Hope

Managing the day-to-day operations of Foster Park Golf Course was one thing—navigating city politics was a whole different beast. For decades, this place had been more than just a golf course. It was where beginners learned the game, retirees found friendship, and families made weekend traditions. It was a gathering place, a piece of the city's heritage.

Then came the flood drainage project. At first, it seemed like just another infrastructure update, nothing to do with us. But when the details came out, it hit me—parts of Foster Park were right in the path of the retention basins and stormwater management zones. I wasn't too worried at first. We'd adjusted before, and the city had always managed to keep the course's character intact.

But this time felt different.

The trucks came in fleets, three separate contractors dropping off hundreds of massive drainage pipes, circling the course like a siege. Then came the digging—excavators carving out 20-foot-deep holes like they were taking bites out of the land. The entrance became a traffic nightmare. Dust, dirt, and danger were everywhere. Business took a huge hit, and there was no end in sight.

As if that weren't enough, the parks department had already hired an architect to draw up a full redesign. I'll admit, it looked impressive, but the price tag was tough to swallow. The plan called for shifting several holes, removing bunkers, and worst of all—eliminating the iconic par-3 6th hole, the one guarded by the towering Foster Park oak. That tree wasn't just part of the course. It was a landmark, a piece of history.

The Parks and Rec club pro pitched the redesign as a necessary modernization—better maintenance, better alignment with the flood project. I wasn't buying it.

And then came the opposition. A small group of residents started making noise, led by two elderly sisters who had lived in the neighborhood forever but had never set foot on the course. They claimed the city didn't need another golf course and questioned why taxpayer money should support it.

"There are plenty of golf courses in Fort Wayne," one of them said at a public hearing. "Why should we maintain this one?"

I sat in the back, listening. They didn't get it. Foster Park wasn't just about golf. It was about community, history, memories passed down through generations.

Someone had to speak up. And that someone was going to be me.

Mac's Plea

At the next city council meeting, I made a beeline for Adam, the head pro for the city park courses. He was scheduled to speak, and I knew he had influence. The chamber was packed—golfers, longtime residents, and city officials, all here to decide the future of Foster Park. My stomach was in knots, but staying silent wasn't an option.

I stepped up to Adam, my voice low but urgent. "I've spent most of my life at Foster Park Golf Course. This place is more than just a golf course. It's where people connect, where kids learn discipline and sportsmanship, where lifelong memories are made. It's been here since 1928—almost a hundred years. Generations of Fort Wayne residents have walked these fairways. It's the most affordable public course we have, and for a lot of people, it's the only one they can afford to play.

"This isn't about fighting progress or flood control. We all understand the need for responsible development. But why does Foster Park have to fight for its survival? This course is a community treasure. It's where high school teams practice, where beginners take their first swing, where veterans find peace. It's where friendships form, where families bond over a shared love of the game."

Adam nodded, then put a hand on my shoulder. "Watch this," he said.

He took his time before speaking, letting the weight of the moment settle over the room. "I'm not here to criticize the hard work of city planners or the architectural firm," he began. "I know they have a job to do. But we need balance—something that respects the needs of the community while preserving the history and character of Foster Park."

His voice softened, a deliberate effort to reach across the aisle. "We're approaching Foster Park's 100th anniversary. That should be a celebration. If changes need to be made, let's do it the right way—with input from the people who cherish this place, who call it home. Let's give this city a course design that will last the next hundred years."

I scanned the room. Some council members looked thoughtful, others unreadable. The two sisters stayed stone-faced. But in the back, I spotted familiar faces—local golfers, high school coaches, neighbors who walked their dogs along the course's tree-lined paths. They nodded in quiet agreement.

I took a deep breath and stepped forward. "I'm asking this council to reconsider. Foster Park isn't just about golf. It's about community, history, and the memories that have shaped this city. Let's work together to protect that legacy for future generations."

As I stepped away from the podium, a wave of uncertainty hit me. I had spoken from the heart. That was all I could do.

The Pro's Dilemma

Adam Thompson paced the small office overlooking the first tee, his frustration obvious. His desk was a mess—maps of the proposed drainage system, budget reports, a public notice about the temporary closure of a few holes at Foster Park. It was supposed to be a short-term inconvenience for long-term gain, but the complaints kept rolling in. Golfers were fed up with limited play, and plenty of them weren't shy about criticizing how the city was handling the project.

I realized why the drainage improvements were necessary. Without them, heavy rains would keep turning the fairways into swamps, making some holes unplayable. But the delays were stacking up, and people were starting to wonder if Foster Park would ever be the same.

Adam ran a hand through his hair, then looked at me. He needed advice, and he knew exactly who to ask.

Seeking Wisdom

I was leaning against the counter in the pro shop, polishing a set of irons, when Adam walked in. He looked tense, his mind clearly running a mile a minute. I glanced up, setting down the club.

"Got a minute, Mac?"

I wiped my hands on a towel. "For you? Always. What's on your mind?"

"It's the drainage project," he said, leaning against the counter. "I believe in the redesign. I know it's going to elevate this place for the next hundred years, but people are upset. They're not seeing the long-term vision—just the inconvenience now. I've got council members breathing down my neck, and some are questioning if it's even worth the hassle. How do I make them see?"

I crossed my arms, looking out the window at the course I knew like the back of my hand. "You're right about the future, Adam. This course deserves more than a patch job. It deserves to stand the test of time, just like it has for nearly a century. But people get stuck in the present. They don't like change, even when it's for the better."

I turned back to him. "You need to remind them what Foster Park means—not just to you or me, but to this community. Paint the picture of what it could be—what it will be. Talk about the high school teams playing on better greens, the families enjoying a round without worrying about rain-soaked fairways. Make them see the legacy we're protecting, not just the inconvenience they're feeling."

Adam nodded, taking it in. I could see the wheels turning.

"And don't just talk about it in meetings," I added. "Get out there on the course. Play a round with the regulars. Show them the problem spots, explain how the drainage work is going to fix them. Let them see your passion firsthand. If they see how much you care, they'll start caring too."

He let out a breath, some of that weight lifting off his shoulders. "You always know how to put things into perspective, Mac."

I chuckled, picking up the iron again and running the cloth over the head. "Been around long enough to know the game's about more than just a ball and a hole. It's about people. Always has been, always will be."

Adam straightened, a spark of determination in his eyes. "You're right. This isn't just about drainage. It's about the next hundred years."

I gave him a small smile. "Then go out there and make them see it. I'll be here, doing my part to keep this place shining."

I watched as he walked out, a renewed sense of purpose in his stride. This fight wasn't just about pipes and turf—it was about preserving something bigger. And neither of us was about to let it slip away.

The Final Loop

It seemed like any other Monday. I got to Foster around 6:00 AM, ready for a steady day. I'd picked up John on the way in, and we set up the clubhouse, stocked the drink coolers, and made sure everything was in place.

The phone rang, and John grabbed it.

"Good morning, Foster Park Golf. This is John. How can I help you? Yeah, he's here. Hold on." He turned to me. "Mac, it's for you."

I took the receiver. "This is Mac."

"Mac, it's Pete! How've you been?"

"Pete!" I said, grinning. "I'm great! You're having a hell of a year. I've been watching you every week—I'm real proud of you. What's up, buddy?"

"Well," he said, "I'm playing in the Open next week in Scotland."

"I know ya are. Hope ya take home the Claret Jug and put Indiana and Fort Wayne on the map."

"Listen, Mac," he said, his tone shifting. "My regular caddie had a death in the family and can't go with me."

"Sorry to hear that," I said. "Scott's been great for you. How can I help? You want me to make some calls, or—"

"No, no, Mac," he cut in. "I want *you* to come be my caddie. All expenses paid, of course, plus 10 percent of my winnings… if I make the cut."

"Oh, you'll make the cut," I told him. "But why would ya want an old geezer like me sharing the spotlight with ya?"

"Here's the thing, Mac," he said. "I wouldn't be here if it weren't for you. You taught me to love this game. You're the best caddie I know. You're my friend for life, and I can't think of anyone I'd rather have on my bag. Please say you'll do it. Please."

I rubbed my jaw, feeling my heart pick up a beat. "Gosh, Pete, ya got me flustered here. Give me till this afternoon. Let me talk it over with Emma, and I'll call ya back by four, okay?"

"Sure," he said.

We hung up, and I went back to my usual routine, but my mind was racing. I'd caddied for a few pros in my time, but *The British Open?* That was another level.

I told John about the offer.

He shook his head. "You'll regret it till the day you die if you don't do it, Mac."

I knew he was right, but I still wanted to talk it over with Emma.

By the time our shift ended, it had been a solid morning. I dropped John off at home.

"So how long's it been since you were in Scotland?" he asked.

"Gosh," I said, thinking, "Not since I was four, maybe five years old."

John smirked. "So about 65 years, huh?"

"Yeah, that sounds about right—and thanks for making me feel ancient."

When I got home, Emma was out in the garden, as usual, hands deep in the dirt. I snuck up behind her and kissed her neck. She jumped.

"Oh! You scared me!"

I grinned. "Now, who else would be lurking back here and kissing you sweetly like that?"

"Only you, Mac. Only you."

"I've got some news and a proposition for ya."

I told her about Pete's call.

She wiped her hands on her jeans and gave me that knowing look. "Well, now, aren't you the one! Of course, you're gonna do it. You have to. He's counting on you. He needs that Mac magic, and you know it."

I tried to downplay my excitement, but she saw right through me—just like always.

"Don't worry, Mac, I'll be fine," she said. "Ginny will come stay with me and bring the grandbabies."

"Are ya sure, babe?"

"Yeah, I'm sure."

The Old Course at St. Andrews—wow. I took a deep breath, letting it sink in. Then I smiled and called Pete.

"I'm in."

"Oh great, Mac! It means the world to me. I'll get the tickets and have yours waiting at the airport. We need to be there Wednesday, so we'll have to leave on Tuesday afternoon. That work for you?"

"Aye, it'll be perfect." I called Foster and told Gerry to mark me off the schedule for a couple of weeks.

"Fine," he said.

Then I got to work. I pulled up the course layout, started a new caddie book, and called Scott. He gave me stock distances for each club—where Pete could play a draw, a fade, or stick one on the green with a one-hop-and-stop.

I'd done plenty of flying when I worked with Titleist, but a 10-hour haul across the Atlantic was a different beast. Pete met me at the airport, and we took a puddle jumper from Fort Wayne to Chicago O'Hare.

When we boarded, I realized he'd booked us in business class. I settled in, watching as 300 people filed on, all headed to the same place. The time difference was six hours, so by the time I landed and got settled… it'd be tomorrow.

Pete ordered us both a cocktail, and when they arrived, I raised my glass and made a toast.

> *"Here's ta Scotland, the land of golf's birth,*
> *Where the winds blow wild and test all yer worth.*
> *To Pete, my lad, ye've come a long way,*
> *From a scrappy wee swing to the Open today.*
> *May yer drives be straight, yer irons be true,*
> *May the bunkers be kind, and the putts roll through.*
> *And if all else fails, and the leaderboard's tight,*
> *We'll toast to the whisky and call it a night!"*

"Thanks, Mac," he said. "I sure am glad you're here."

And off we went. It wasn't long before we reached cruising altitude. I took my caddie book from my carry-on bag and showed it to Pete.

"Impressive," he said.

"Not as much as I'd like," I replied. "We got some work to do."

"Scotland's weather can go from sunny to shit in a minute," I told him. "I'll be up at the crack of dawn to get the forecast each day, and I'm headed to the course as soon as we arrive to mark some distances I don't have yet."

We settled in, and Pete asked me about Emma and the kids. I assured him all was good, and we each traded some stories.

Pete leaned back in his seat, the hum of the airplane engines a soothing backdrop, and turned to me with a grin.

"You know, Mac, I wasn't always the composed player you see today," Pete said, his eyes twinkling with mischief. "Back when I was first starting to play in tournaments, I had a moment that still makes me cringe—and laugh."

I raised an eyebrow. "Oh, aye? This I've got to hear."

Pete chuckled. "It was my first local junior championship. I was barely sixteen, still figuring out how to hold my nerves together on the course. By some miracle, I was leading going into the final day, paired with the best player in town—a guy everyone called 'Big Sam.' And let me tell you, Mac, Sam was intimidating. He was built like a linebacker and had a booming drive to match. I was half his size and twice as nervous."

I smiled knowingly. "Pressure's a cruel teacher, lad."

"That it is," Pete agreed. "So, we're on the 17th hole, a long par five, and I've got a one-shot lead. Big Sam cranks a monster drive straight down the middle—classic Sam. I step up, trying to stay calm, and just as I'm about to swing, I hear this buzzing sound. At first, I thought it was in my head, like nerves or something. But then, out of nowhere, a huge bumblebee lands on my hat."

I let out a deep laugh. "Ach, no!"

"Yes!" Pete said, laughing. "It's just sitting there, buzzing away, and I can feel the crowd watching, waiting. Someone in the gallery whispers, 'Don't move!' and now I'm frozen, holding my driver like a statue. Big Sam is doubled over laughing, and the marshals don't know what to do. It's chaos."

"So what did you do, lad?" I asked, grinning.

"Well," Pete said, leaning in conspiratorially, "I panicked. I took my hat off slowly, praying it wouldn't sting me, and I held it out like I was offering the bee as a gift to the golf gods. The thing finally flew off, but I was so rattled that my drive hooked hard left—right into the middle of the parking lot."

I slapped my knee, roaring with laughter. "Did you lose the tournament?"

"Not quite," Pete said, grinning. "I scrambled for par on the last hole and forced a playoff. But Big Sam had the upper hand by then and took me down. Afterward, he said to me, 'Pete, next time, wear a bee-proof hat.'"

I shook my head, laughing. "Well, lad, if nothing else, you learned how to handle a bit of pressure—and a lot of buzzing nonsense!"

Pete nodded, his expression softening. Then it was my turn.

I leaned back in my seat, gazing out the window at the endless clouds. After a moment of quiet, I turned to Pete, a sly smile playing on my lips.

"You know, lad, there was a time I learned the hard way that pride can be as dangerous as a bunker on a windy day."

Pete raised an eyebrow. "Oh, this sounds like a good one."

"It was back when I was caddying as a young man," I began. "There was a regular at Fort Wayne Country Club—Mr. Grayson. Wealthy fella, always dressed to the nines. He had a golf game to match—or so he thought. Grayson loved to show off, especially when his business mates were in town. And he had a bit of a temper when things didn't go his way."

Pete chuckled. "Sounds like a charmer."

"Aye," I said. "One fine Saturday, Grayson invites a big-shot client for a round. He's out to impress, naturally, and he's having a decent game—until we get to the 14th hole. It's a tricky dogleg left with a creek running through it. Grayson hits his ball straight into the water."

Pete winced. "Oof."

"That's not the half of it," I said. "He insists on finding his ball. So there we are, wading through the muck—Grayson in his shiny white trousers, swearing up a storm. Finally, he spots it—a glint of white in the mud—and says, 'I, fetch me my 7-iron. I'm going to play it from here.'"

Pete's jaw dropped. "In the creek? No way."

"Oh, aye," I said, shaking my head. "I tried to talk him out of it. Told him he'd never make the green, that he'd ruin his trousers and his day. But Grayson was too proud to listen. So I handed him the 7-iron and stepped back."

Pete leaned in, grinning. "What happened?"

"Grayson takes a mighty swing, mud flying everywhere. He doesn't just miss the ball—he loses his balance, falls flat on his back in the creek, and sends his club sailing into the bushes. His client is trying not to laugh, I'm biting my cheek to keep a straight face, and Grayson is lying there, soaked and sputtering, looking like a drowned rat."

Pete burst out laughing. "What did he do?"

"He got up, covered in mud, and said, 'Mac, let's just call that one a wash.' Then he walked straight to the clubhouse without finishing the round."

Pete was laughing so hard, tears were forming in his eyes. "That's brilliant, Mac. Did he ever live it down?"

"He came back the next week, acting like nothing happened. But every time he reached for his 7-iron, I'd give him a look, and he'd glare at me like I'd said something. Never did try a creek shot again, though."

Pete shook his head, still chuckling. "So, what's the lesson there, Mac? Don't let pride sink you?"

"Aye, that's part of it," I said. "But it's also this: Sometimes, we make a mess of things, and the best thing to do is laugh, clean ourselves up, and keep playing. Grayson taught me that, though I doubt he realized it at the time."

I leaned back in my seat and said, "Golf's like that, Pete—full of moments that make fools of us but also remind us we're human. You just have to keep swinging, no matter the muck."

Pete nodded, his smile fading into a thoughtful expression. "That's why I'm lucky to have you as my caddie, Mac. You've got a story—and a lesson—for everything."

I gave him a wink. "Aye, lad. And in Scotland, you'll see—we're just getting started."

We both nodded off until the pilot announced we were making our final approach. "Prepare for landing."

Chapter 9

St. Andrew's

The flight had been long, but the fatigue melted away the moment we stepped onto the grounds of St. Andrews. We stood side by side, me with Pete's bags slung over my shoulder, gazing at the sprawling links before us. The salty breeze carried the faint sound of seagulls, and the ancient stone buildings of the town stood like sentinels, whispering stories of centuries past.

"Pete, would you look at this," I murmured, my voice soft with reverence. My gaze swept across the expanse of rolling fairways and fescue, each blade of grass seeming to hold a piece of history. "The Home of Golf. We're standing where Old Tom Morris himself once walked."

Pete nodded, silent for a moment, his eyes wide as they took in the sight of the iconic Swilcan Bridge, the sharp edges of the Road

Hole bunker, and the sprawling 18th green that seemed to blend seamlessly into the horizon.

"It's… it's incredible," he finally said, his voice barely above a whisper. "I've seen it on TV a hundred times, but being here… it's like stepping into a painting. Or a dream."

I chuckled, a deep, warm sound that carried a hint of awe. "Aye, lad. This isn't just a golf course—it's hallowed ground. Every blade of grass, every bunker, every stone in these walls has seen greatness. They've stood witness to the best and worst of this game we love."

He gestured toward the first tee, where a group of players was preparing to start their round. "Think of all the legends who've stood right there. Jack Nicklaus, Seve Ballesteros, Bobby Jones… and now, Pete Myers."

Pete let out a nervous laugh, rubbing the back of his neck. "No pressure, right?"

I clapped a reassuring hand on his shoulder. "No pressure at all. Just the whole world watching. But don't you worry, lad. You've got the game, and you've got me."

We started walking toward the practice area, the crunch of gravel beneath their feet mingling with the distant thwack of irons meeting balls. I couldn't help but glance around, taking in the centuries-old stone walls and the timeless beauty of the links.

"When I was a boy back in Scotland," I said in a quiet voice, "I used to dream about places like this. To me, St. Andrews wasn't just a course; it was an idea, a symbol of everything good about the game. And now, here I am. It feels like coming home in a way, doesn't it?"

Pete nodded again, his expression a mix of awe and determination. "It does. But it's also humbling. I feel like I'm standing in the shadow of giants."

All I could do was smile, knowing there was a twinkle in my eye. "Aye, but giants were once just men, Pete. And one of them might be you, lad. You've earned your place here, and don't you forget it."

As we reached the edge of the Old Course, I paused to take a deep breath, letting the crisp air fill my lungs.

"You know, Pete," I said, my voice softer now, "St. Andrews has a way of reminding you what this game is all about. Not just winning or losing, but the beauty of it, the camaraderie, the lessons it teaches us about life."

Pete looked out over the course, the waves of the North Sea glinting in the distance. "I get it, Mac. This is more than a tournament. It's a privilege."

"Aye," I agreed. "It's the privilege of walking the same fairways as the greats, of adding your name to the story of this place. And no matter what happens this week, just remember—you're part of that history now."

Pete nodded, his expression resolute. "Thanks, Mac. Let's make it a good one."

With a shared smile, we turned toward the course, the weight of its history settling on our shoulders but lifting our spirits. We were here, at St. Andrews—the birthplace of golf, the theater of dreams—and we were both ready to play our part in its history.

The Open Championship at St. Andrews

The wind carried the salt of the North Sea as Pete and I stepped onto the first tee at St. Andrews. This was sacred ground, where legends had walked, where golf had been shaped over centuries. Pete exhaled, gripping his driver, and I, stood beside him with the bag slung over his shoulder, I leaned in.

"Aye, lad," I said, my Scottish brogue thick with meaning. "Welcome to the Home of Golf."

Round 1 – A Nervous Start

Pete's first shot of the tournament wasn't perfect. His drive leaked right, settling in the thick fescue. The nerves were real, and I could see it in his eyes.

"Don't force it," I said. "Play smart. The Old Course will punish impatience."

Pete scrambled for par but bogeyed the next hole. He steadied himself with a birdie on the 5th, and by the back nine, he started finding his rhythm. The swirling winds made club selection a guessing game, and my experience proved invaluable.

On the infamous 17th, the Road Hole, Pete's approach shot landed dangerously close to the stone wall behind the green. I gave him a knowing nod. "Could be worse, lad. At least ye didnae hit the Jigger Inn."

Pete managed to escape with bogey and finished the round at even par—respectable, but not spectacular. He was tied for 24th, knowing he'd have to do better.

Round 2 – Finding His Game

The second round started in the morning mist, the links stretching endlessly before them. Pete, more comfortable now, attacked the course with confidence.

He reached the 14th, the longest hole on the course, his drive was amazing. It caught the hill and traveled 40 more yards, leaving about 255 from his approach.

Needing a big moment, I handed him a 3-wood. "Give it a rip, but keep it out the gorse."

Pete crushed it, the ball rolling onto the green, setting up an eagle putt. When he drained it, the crowd erupted, and I gave him a rare grin. "Aye, lad. Now you're playin' golf."

The 17th was kinder this time, and Pete finished with a 68, climbing to 10th place. He was in the hunt.

Round 3 – Moving Day Drama

Saturday was where champions made their moves. Pete started hot, making three birdies in the first six holes. By the turn, he had climbed into the top five.

Then came the 11th hole, where a sudden gust of wind sent his tee shot sailing into a deep pot bunker. I walked up, peering into the sandy grave. "Well, lad, you wanted a challenge."

Pete blasted out, the ball barely clearing the lip, and he managed to save bogey.

The defining moment came on the 18th. Needing a birdie to stay in the final pairing, Pete faced a 30-foot putt over the Valley of Sin. I knelt, reading the break carefully.

"Hit it firm, let it take the slope."

Pete stroked the putt. It trickled down the ridge, slowed, and disappeared into the cup. The crowd roared. He was tied for second, heading into Sunday with a real chance at history.

Final Round – The Battle for the Claret Jug

Sunday at St. Andrews

The weight of the moment was immense. Pete stepped onto the first tee beside his playing partner—a former major champion and the favorite to win. The sun was bright, the wind light but unpredictable. The Open was there for the taking.

Pete played steady but trailed by two shots at the turn. On the 12th, he drained a clutch birdie while the leader faltered with a bogey.

By the time they reached 17, the Road Hole awaited, and Pete was tied for the lead. His drive was safe, but his approach came up just short. The leader missed his par putt, opening the door.

I handed Pete his putter and murmured, "Ya know what to do."

Pete steadied himself, took his stance, and rolled the ball perfectly. It curled toward the cup, hesitated—then lipped out. Agonizingly close. He tapped in for par. They were tied going into 18.

Pete stood on the final tee, trailing by a single stroke. The grandstands were packed, the North Sea wind swirling, the sun casting a golden glow over the historic course. I stood beside him, arms crossed, calm as ever.

"One more good swing, lad," I said. "Trust yerself."

Pete took a deep breath and swung. The ball soared, landing center fairway. As he and I walked down the final hole, the roar of the crowd and the weight of history surrounded us.

His approach shot landed just off the green. The leader made par. Pete needed to hole his chip to force a playoff.

He studied the shot—I stood beside him, silent, knowing there was nothing left to say.

Pete swung. The ball rolled beautifully, tracking toward the hole. The crowd held its breath. It slowed… slowed… and stopped inches short.

He tapped in for par. The tournament was over. He finished second. So close, but not quite.

The Aftermath – More Than a Trophy

As Pete stepped off the green, devastation washed over him. I rested a hand on his shoulder.

"You didn't lose today, lad. You arrived."

Reporters swarmed. Cameras flashed.

"Pete, how does it feel to come up just short?" a journalist asked.

Pete looked around—at the Old Course, the cheering fans, the kids leaning over the ropes for autographs. He smiled.

"I didn't come up short," Pete said. "I just proved that I belong here."

The celebration that evening was nothing short of grand. The clubhouse buzzed with laughter and clinking glasses, a mix of players, caddies, and families sharing stories of the week. Pete stood in the center, his face still flush from the whirlwind of it all. Then, across the room, I saw her—Emma, standing by the window, watching me with a proud, knowing smile.

I made my way to her, slipping my hand into hers. "Didn't expect to see you here, love."

"Where else would I be?" she said, squeezing my hand. "He's not the only one who made it here, Mac."

We stepped outside, the distant echoes of celebration fading behind us. The night air was crisp, the scent of the sea lingering in the breeze. As we strolled through St. Andrews, we stopped at the famous Swilcan Bridge. I ran a hand over the worn stone, my fingers tracing history itself.

"You know, Pete," I said, looking out over the darkened course, "Winning's grand. But leaving your mark? That's what really matters."

Pete nodded, eyes scanning the fairways, knowing this was just the beginning.

I watched him go, the young man disappearing into the night, his stride steady, his head high.

Emma tugged my arm gently. "Proud of him, aren't you?"

I exhaled, a slow, thoughtful breath. "Aye. More than he knows."

We continued walking, the streets quiet, the town settling into the hush of late evening. I glanced at Emma, at the lines time had carved into both our faces.

"You know," I said, "I spent my whole life chasing moments like this. But standing here, with you, I reckon this is the best one of all."

Emma smiled, leaning into me as we walked on, leaving footprints on the old stone path—just another mark in the long story of the game we loved.

C H A P T E R 10

The Open Was My Last Loop

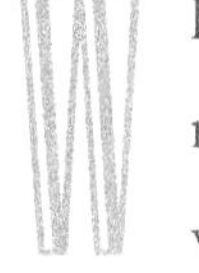hen I returned to Foster, you'd have thought I was a celebrity. John had arranged a catered celebration. All the regulars were there, plus the guys from St. John's Mafia.

★★★

The Highs and Lows of Caddying

I leaned against the pro shop counter, arms crossed, watching the young man in front of me shift nervously from foot to foot. The kid—sixteen, maybe younger—had that restless energy I had seen before. Wide-eyed, full of big dreams, and no clue what he was in for.

"So," I said, tilting my head, "You think you want to be a caddie?"

"Yes, sir," the boy answered quickly. "I love golf, and I figure it's a good way to make money and meet players."

I chuckled, shaking my head. "Loving golf's got nothing to do with it, kid. You're not playing—you're carrying the bag, watching someone else hit the shots. And meeting players? Sure. Some you'll like. Some you'll wish you never met. You still want the job?"

The kid hesitated, then nodded.

"Alright," I said, leaning forward. "Let me tell you a few things about this life—the good and the bad. Then you'll see if you've really got what it takes."

★★★

The First Real Test

"My first loop, I thought I was gonna die. The bag was too heavy, the sun was too hot, and my golfer—some businessman who thought he was playing for a green jacket—acted like I was invisible unless he needed me to pull the pin or clean a club. By the third hole, my shoulders burned. By the ninth, my legs felt like jelly. And then came the back nine, where I learned the golden rule of caddying: you don't show weakness. You don't drop the bag, you don't complain, and you sure as hell don't sit down. If you do, they'll never call your name again. I made it, barely. But that night, I collapsed onto my bed and swore I'd never caddie again. By morning, I was back at the course, waiting for my next loop."

★★★

The Highs – When You Get It Right

"When you do the job right, when you really start to understand it—that's when it gets good. There was this one round—Kenny was playing, and I was on his bag. We were in a tight match, and he had a tricky downhill putt on 17. He called me over. 'Mac, what do you see?' I took my time, crouched down, felt the slope with my feet, let my gut take over. 'Inside right,' I said. 'Firm stroke.' He stared at the line, then at me, then back at the ball. He trusted me. And damn if he didn't roll that putt right into the heart of the cup. That feeling? Knowing you made a difference? Knowing you earned your golfer's trust? That's a high you can't buy."

The Lows – When It All Goes Wrong

"Of course, it doesn't always go that way. One time, I was caddying for a guy with a real shot at winning a local tournament. Last hole, fairway, one shot off the lead. He asked me for a club. I was sure it was an 8-iron. Told him so with confidence. He flushed it—cleanest strike he'd hit all day. Ball sailed over the green, took a nasty bounce, and ended up in the parking lot. Out of bounds. Tournament lost. He didn't say a word. Just stared at that parking lot like it had personally betrayed him. I learned two lessons that day. One, there's nothing worse than knowing you just cost someone a win. And two—when in doubt, take one less club."

The Characters You Meet

"You meet all kinds out there. The generous ones who slip you an extra twenty just for keeping up. The tightwads who act like they're doing you a favor by letting you carry their bag. The talkers who tell you their life story. The silent types who won't say a word—unless they're yelling about a missed putt. And then, there are the real characters. Like old Mr. Callahan, who swore every missed putt was my fault because I didn't 'read the wind right.' Or Eddie the Dentist, who bet on every shot and made me his personal good-luck charm—until the day he lost. Then, suddenly, I was 'bad juju.'"

So, You Still Want the Job?

I leaned back, watching the kid take it all in.

"The truth is, caddying is a grind. You wake up early, walk miles every day, and deal with people who think their six-dollar golf ball matters more than your time. But it's also a front-row seat to the best moments in the game. You see incredible shots up close, learn from guys who live and breathe golf, and if you're good—really good—you earn their respect. And if you're lucky, like I was, maybe it even takes you places you never imagined."

The kid thought for a moment, then squared his shoulders. "Sounds tough. But I think I still want to try."

I grinned. "Good. Be here at five-thirty tomorrow. Let's see if you've got what it takes."

CHAPTER 11

The Next Hoosier Caddie

The first time I saw him, I knew.

He stood at the edge of the practice green, shifting nervously from foot to foot, hands shoved deep into his pockets. He was about fifteen, maybe sixteen—lean, lanky, with a mop of dark hair poking out from under his cap. His eyes darted across the course, taking everything in—the way the older men rolled putts across the green, the chatter of golfers stepping off the 18th, the hum of carts in the distance.

He wasn't just watching. He was studying.

I saw myself in that boy.

I leaned against the pro shop doorframe, arms crossed. "Looking for something, kid?"

He turned quickly, startled. "Uh, no—I mean… yeah, maybe." He hesitated, then sighed. "I was hoping to find a job. I heard you used to have caddies here, but I guess not anymore."

I gave him a long look. "Not for a long time. You play?"

"A little," he admitted. "My grandpa used to take me to the range when I was a kid, but we don't really have the money for me to play much."

I nodded. "Golf's an expensive game. But it's also a game that can give back if you know where to look."

He met my gaze, curiosity flickering beneath his uncertainty.

"You ever hear of the Evans Scholarship?" I asked.

He shook his head.

I grinned. "Well then, kid, we've got some work to do."

A Lesson in Golf and Life

His name was Lucas, but everyone just called him Luke.

He started coming around after school, first just helping out—picking up range balls, stocking drinks in the pro shop, watching the regulars. But I knew what he really wanted. He wanted to be out there, where the game was played, where the lessons were learned.

So one evening, after I closed up shop, I handed him an old set of clubs. "Meet me at the first tee."

Luke soaked up every word, every tip, every piece of advice. At first, he swung too hard, trying to muscle the ball down the fairway like most young players do.

"It's not about power," I told him as we stood beneath the fading light one evening. "It's about rhythm. Feel the club, let it do the work."

He frowned, adjusting his grip. "Like a dance?"

I chuckled. "Exactly. But don't tell the other guys I said that."

Little by little, he got better. His putting became sharp, his short game precise. But more importantly, he started to understand the game—not just the mechanics, but the patience, the respect, the etiquette. The things that separate a golfer from just a guy who hits a ball.

The Round That Changed Everything

The first time he played a full round with me, I caddied for him.

It was a crisp autumn morning, the fairways still wet with dew.

"You're the player today," I told him, handing him his driver. "I'll be your caddie. You tell me what you're thinking, and I'll tell you if you're thinking wrong."

He smirked. "Sounds fair."

The round wasn't about his score—it was about his decisions. He laid up when he needed to, played the percentages, didn't let a bad shot rattle him. He was learning.

By the time we reached the 18th, he was standing over a ten-foot putt for par. He looked at me. "Left edge?"

I grinned. "You tell me."

He studied the green, took his stance, and stroked the putt with quiet confidence. The ball curled perfectly into the cup.

I clapped him on the back. "You're getting it, Luke."

A Future Earned

The Evans Scholarship wasn't a given. He had to earn it—not just with his game, but with his character, his grades, his work ethic.

I helped him apply, just like my old caddie master had helped me all those years ago. We filled out forms, gathered recommendations. I told him what to expect in the interview—the questions, the scrutiny, the weight of it all.

"You think I have a chance?" he asked one evening as we sat on the pro shop porch, watching the last golfers finish their rounds.

I looked him in the eye. "I know you do. But you have to believe it too."

A few months later, the letter arrived.

Luke showed up at the course, breathless, waving the envelope in the air. He didn't have to say anything. I could see it in his eyes.

"You're looking at the newest Evans Scholar," he said, his voice cracking with excitement.

I pulled him into a hug. "You earned it, kid."

The Final Round

On his last day before heading off to college, we played one final round together.

Walking up the 18th fairway, he turned to me. "Mac, do you ever think about what would've happened if you hadn't gotten the scholarship? If you never became a caddie?"

I nodded, letting the question settle. "I think about it all the time. But golf has a way of leading you where you're meant to go."

He smiled. "Well, I hope it leads me back here someday."

I patted him on the back. "It always does."

That evening, long after Luke had left, I walked the course alone. The air had that late-summer heaviness, the kind that lingers before autumn sets in.

I found myself at the first tee, running my hand over the weathered wooden bench where I had sat so many times before—watching, waiting, learning.

Funny how the game gives back. How it teaches, shapes, and guides us.

I had spent a lifetime on these fairways, watching young men take their first swings, stumble, rise again. Some made it big. Some just found a love for the game that never faded.

And some—like Luke—walked the same path I once did.

I smiled, tipping my cap to the empty fairway.

"See you out there, kid."